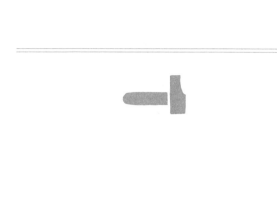

Published by Creative Education, Inc.
123 South Broad Street, Mankato, Minnesota 56001.

Designed by Rita Marshall
Cover Illustration by Roberto Innocenti

Acknowledgment: Copyright The William Saroyan
Foundation

Library of Congress Cataloging-in-Publication Data

Saroyan, William, 1908–
    The parsley garden/by William Saroyan.
    p.   cm.
    Summary: After being caught shoplifting, eleven-
year-old Al feels humiliated and tries to recapture his
self-respect.
    ISBN 0-88682-355-2
    [1. Shoplifting—Fiction.   2. Self-respect—
Fiction.]   I. Title.
PZ7.S2485Par   1990
[Fic]—dc20   90-2079
                                              CIP
                                              AC

THE
PARSLEY GARDEN

WILLIAM SAROYAN

CREATIVE EDUCATION INC.

ONE DAY IN AUGUST AL CONDRAJ WAS

WANDERING THROUGH WOOLWORTH'S

without a penny to spend when he saw a small

hammer that was not a toy but a real hammer,

and he was possessed with a longing to have it. He

believed it was just what he needed by which to

break the monotony and with which to make

something. He had gathered some first-class

nails from Foley's Packing House where the

boxmakers worked and where they had

carelessly dropped at least fifteen cents' worth.

He had gladly gone to the trouble of gathering

them together because it had seemed to him that

a nail, as such, was not something to be wasted.

He had the nails, perhaps a half pound of them,

at least two hundred of them, in a paper bag in

the apple box in which he kept his junk at home.

Now, with the ten-cent hammer he believed he could make something out of box wood and the nails, although he had no idea what. Some sort of a table perhaps, or a small bench.

At any rate he took the hammer and slipped it into the pocket of his overalls, but just as he did so a man took him firmly by the arm without a word and pushed him to the back of the store into a small office. Another man, an older one, was seated behind a desk in the office, working with papers. The younger man, the one who had captured him, was excited and his forehead was covered with sweat.

"Well," he said, "here's one more of them."

The man behind the desk got to his feet and looked Al Condraj up and down.

"What's *he* swiped?"

"A hammer." The young man looked at Al with hatred. "Hand it over," he said.

The boy brought the hammer out of his

pocket and handed it to the young man, who said, "I ought to hit you over the head with it, that's what I ought to do."

He turned to the older man, the boss, the manager of the store, and he said, "What do you want me to do with him?"

"Leave him with me," the older man said.

The younger man stepped out of the office, and the older man sat down and went back to work. Al Condraj stood in the office fifteen minutes before the older man looked at him again.

"Well," he said.

Al didn't know what to say. The man wasn't looking at him, he was looking at the door.

Finally Al said, "I didn't mean to steal it. I just need it and I haven't got any money."

"Just because you haven't got any money doesn't mean you've got a right to steal things," the man said. "Now, does it?"

"No, sir."

"Well, what am I going to do with you? Turn you over to the police?"

Al didn't say anything, but he certainly didn't want to be turned over to the police. He hated the man, but at the same time he realized some-body else could be a lot tougher than he was being.

"If I let you go, will you promise never to steal from this store again?"

"Yes, sir."

"All right," the man said. "Go out this way and don't come back to this store until you've got some money to spend."

He opened a door to the hall that led to the alley, and Al Condraj hurried down the hall and out into the alley.

The first thing he did when he was free was laugh, but he knew he had been humiliated, and he was deeply ashamed. It was not in his nature to take things that did not belong to him. He hated the young man who had caught him and he hated the manager of the store who had made him stand in silence in the office so long. He hadn't liked it at all when the young man had said he ought to hit him over the head with the hammer.

He should have had the courage to look him straight in the eye and say, "You and who else?"

Of course he *had* stolen the hammer and he had been caught, but it seemed to him he oughtn't to have been so humiliated.

After he had walked three blocks he decided he didn't want to go home just yet, so he turned around and started walking back to town. He almost believed he meant to go back and say something to the young man who had caught him. And then he wasn't sure he didn't mean to go back and steal the hammer again, and this time *not* get caught. As long as he had been made to feel like a thief anyway, the least he ought to get out of it was the hammer.

Outside the store he lost his nerve, though. He stood in the street, looking in, for at least ten minutes.

Then, crushed and confused and now bitterly ashamed of himself, first for having stolen something, then for having been caught, then for having been humiliated, then for not having guts enough to go back and do the job right, he began walking home again, his mind so troubled that he didn't greet his pal Pete Wawchek when they came face to face outside Graf's Hardware.

When he got home he was too ashamed to go inside and examine his junk, so he had a long drink of water from the faucet in the backyard. The faucet was used by his mother to water the stuff she planted every year: okra, bell peppers, tomatoes, cucumbers, onions, garlic, mint, eggplants, and parsley.

His mother called the whole business the parsley garden, and every night in the summer she would bring chairs out of the house and put them around the table she had had Ondro, the neighborhood handyman, make for her for fifteen cents, and she would sit at the table and enjoy the cool of the garden and the smell of the things she had planted and tended.

Sometimes she would even make a salad and moisten the flat old-country bread and slice some white cheese, and she and he would have supper in the parsley garden. After supper she would attach the water hose to the faucet and water her plants and the place would be cooler than ever and it would smell real good, real fresh and cool and green, all the different growing things making a green garden smell out of themselves and the air and the water.

After the long drink of water he sat down where the parsley itself was growing and he pulled a handful of it out and slowly ate it. Then he went inside and told his mother what had happened. He even told her what he had *thought* of doing after he had been turned loose: to go back and steal the hammer again.

"I don't want you to steal," his mother said in broken English. "Here is ten cents. You go back to that man and you give him this money and you bring it home, that hammer."

"No," Al Condraj said. "I won't take your money for something I don't really need. I just thought I ought to have a hammer, so I could make something if I felt like it. I've got a lot of nails and some box wood, but I haven't got a hammer."

"Go buy it, that hammer," his mother said.

"No," Al said.

"All right," his mother said. "Shut up."

That's what she always said when she didn't know what else to say.

Al went out and sat on the steps. His humiliation was beginning to really hurt now. He decided to wander off along the railroad tracks to

Foley's because he needed to think about it some more. At Foley's he watched Johnny Gale nailing boxes for ten minutes, but Johnny was too busy to notice him or talk to him, although one day at Sunday school, two or three years ago, Johnny had greeted him and said, "How's the boy?" Johnny worked with a boxmaker's hatchet and everybody in Fresno said he was the fastest boxmaker in town. He was the clos-est thing to a machine any packing house ever saw. Foley himself was proud of Johnny Gale.

Al Condraj finally set out for home because

he didn't want to get in the way. He didn't want somebody working hard to notice that he was being watched and maybe say to him, "Go on, beat it." He didn't want Johnny Gale to do something like that. He didn't want to invite another humiliation.

On the way home he looked for money but all he found was the usual pieces of broken glass and rusty nails, the things that were always cutting his bare feet every summer.

When he got home his mother had made a salad and set the table, so he sat down to eat, but when he put the food in his mouth he just didn't care for it. He got up and went into the three-room house and got his apple box out of the corner of his room and went through his junk. It was all there, the same as yesterday.

He wandered off back to town and stood in front of the closed store, hating the young man who had caught him, and then he went along to the Hippodrome and looked at the display photographs from the two movies that were being shown that day.

Then he went along to the public library to

have a look at all the books again, but he didn't like any of them, so he wandered around town some more, and then around half past eight he went home and went to bed.

His mother had already gone to bed because she had to be up at five to go to work at Inderrieden's, packing figs. Some days there would be work all day, some days there would be only half a day of it, but whatever his mother earned during the summer had to keep them the whole year.

He didn't sleep much that night because he

couldn't get over what had happened, and he went over six or seven ways by which to adjust the matter. He went so far as to believe it would be necessary to kill the young man who had caught him. He also believed it would be necessary for him to steal systematically and successfully the rest of his life. It was a hot night and he couldn't sleep.

Finally, his mother got up and walked barefooted to the kitchen for a drink of water and on the way back she said to him softly, "Shut up."

When she got up at five in the morning he was out of the house, but that had happened many times before. He was a restless boy, and he kept moving all the time every summer. He was making mistakes and paying for them, and he had just tried stealing and had been caught at it, and he was troubled. She fixed her breakfast, packed her lunch, and hurried off to work, hoping it would be a full day.

It was a full day, and then there was overtime, and although she had no more lunch she decided to work on for the extra money, anyway.

Almost all the other packers were staying on, too, and her neighbor across the alley, Leeza Ahboot, who worked beside her, said, "Let us work until the work stops, then we'll go home and fix a supper between us and eat it in your parsley garden where it's so cool. It's a hot day and there's no sense not making an extra fifty or sixty cents."

When the two women reached the garden it was almost nine o'clock, but still daylight, and she saw her son nailing pieces of box wood together, making something with a hammer. It looked like a bench. He had already watered the garden and tidied up the rest of the yard, and the place seemed very nice, and her son seemed very serious and busy. She and Leeza went straight to work for their supper, picking bell peppers and tomatoes and cucumbers and a great deal of parsley for the salad.

Then Leeza went to her house for some bread which she had baked the night before, and some white cheese, and in a few minutes they were having supper together and talking pleasantly about the successful day they had had. After supper, they made Turkish coffee over an open fire in the yard. They drank the coffee and smoked a cigarette apiece, and told one another stories about their experiences in the old country and here in Fresno, and then they looked into their cups at the grounds to see if any good fortune was indicated, and there was: health and work and supper out of doors in the summer and enough money for the rest of the year.

Al Condraj worked and overheard some of the things they said, and then Leeza went home to go to bed, and his mother said, "Where you get it, that hammer, Al?"

"I got it at the store."

"How you get it? You steal it?"

Al Condraj finished the bench and sat on it.

"No," he said. "I didn't steal it."

"How you get it?"

"I worked at the store for it," Al said.

"The store where you steal it yesterday?"

"Yes."

"Who give you job?"

"The boss."

"What you do?"

"I carried different stuff to the different counters."

"Well, that's good," the woman said. "How long you work for that little hammer?"

"I worked all day," Al said. "Mr. Clemmer gave me the hammer after I'd worked one hour, but I went right on working. The fellow who caught me yesterday showed me what to do, and we worked together. We didn't talk, but at the end of the day he took me to Mr. Clemmer's office and he told Mr. Clemmer that I'd worked hard all day and ought to be paid at least a dollar."

"That's good," the woman said.

"So Mr. Clemmer put a silver dollar on his desk for me, and then the fellow who caught me yesterday told him the store needed a boy like me every day, for a dollar a day, and Mr. Clemmer said I could have the job."

"That's good," the woman said. "You can make it a little money for yourself."

"I left the dollar on Mr. Clemmer's desk," Al Condraj said, "and I told them both I didn't want the job."

"Why you say that?" the woman said. "Dollar a day for eleven-year-old boy good money. Why you not take job?"

"Because I hate the both of them," the boy said. "I would never work for people like that. I just looked at them and picked up my hammer and walked out. I came home and I made this bench."

"All right," his mother said. "Shut up."

His mother went inside and went to bed, but Al Condraj sat on the bench he had made and smelled the parsley garden and didn't feel humiliated anymore.

But nothing could stop him from hating the two men, even though he knew they hadn't done anything they shouldn't have done.